**FRIENDS
OF ACPL**

 WALKER AND COMPANY / New York

WHATEVER HAPPENED

By PHYLLIS GOLDMAN and GRACE JAFFE

Illustrated by ART SEIDEN

Nina and Joshua live in a tall apartment in a big city.
Nina is seven and her brother, Joshua, is four.
Every afternoon, Nina and Joshua and their Mother go
   to the park—
Or to the zoo—
Or walk down the avenue looking in the different
   store windows.

KEEP OFF THE GRASS

Every morning, Nina goes to school.
Joshua stays home with his Mother while she cleans the house.
When Joshua's Mother said, "Please put away your truck;
I have to vacuum the rug."

Joshua said, "No."
Later, Mother said, "Please wash your hands, Josh, it's time
    for lunch."
And Joshua said, "No, no."

That night, Daddy said, "It's time for your bath, Josh."
And Joshua said, "No, no, no."
"Oh dear," sighed Mother.
"My, my," said Daddy, sternly.

"Gee whiz," said Nina. "Joshua has lost the word YES.
  Where can it be?"
Joshua shrugged his shoulders. "I don't know," he said.

Let's help Joshua find it.
Mother looked in the shiny
    white bathtub—
But it wasn't there.

Daddy searched the cool, green fish bowl—
But it wasn't there.

And Joshua peeked into his crowded toy chest—
But it wasn't there. It wasn't anywhere.

So they looked some more.
They looked in the big piano,

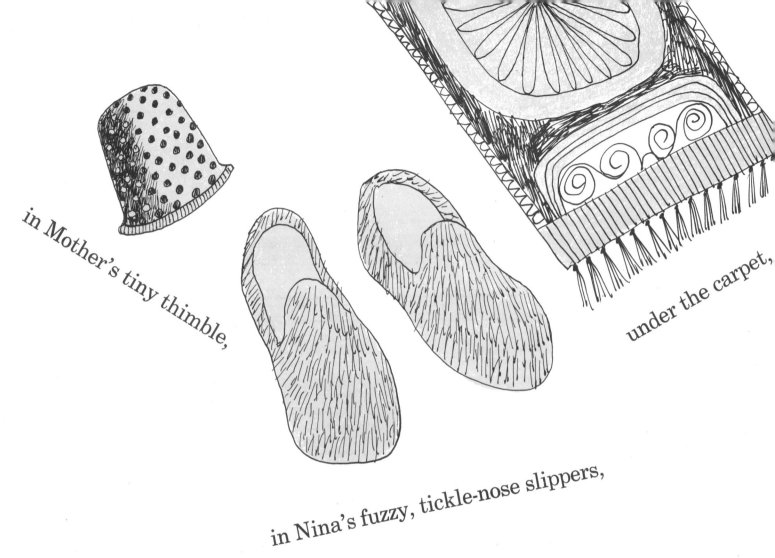

in Mother's tiny thimble,

in Nina's fuzzy, tickle-nose slippers,

under the carpet,

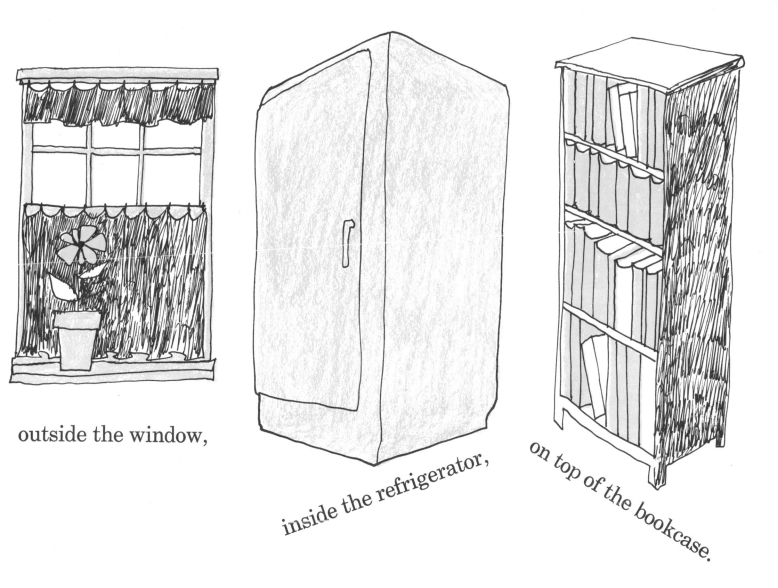

outside the window,

inside the refrigerator,

on top of the bookcase.

But it wasn't there. It wasn't anywhere.

Suddenly, Joshua burst out laughing.

"What is it?" asked Nina.

"*I* know where it is, I know where it is," he said.

"I've had it all along."

"Where is it?" asked Mother and Daddy and Nina.

"It's right in here," said Joshua. "It's been
hiding here *all the time*."
And sure enough, Joshua opened his mouth and
what do you think he could say?

Big yeses and little yeses,
loud yeses and soft yeses,
happy yeses and I-don't-want-to-
but-I-will yeses,
and all sorts of different yeses.

Now, when Mother asks Joshua to put away his paints—
Or Nina asks Joshua to help find her lost ball—
Or Daddy asks Joshua to brush his teeth before bedtime—
Joshua almost always answers, "YES."

Everyone is so glad that Joshua
has found "yes" again.
Have *you* ever lost YES?
Open your mouth V E R Y slowly
and maybe it will be hiding
there for you, too.

Text Copyright ● 1970 by Phyllis Goldman and Grace Jaffe

Illustrations Copyright ● 1970 by Art Seiden

First published in the United States of America in 1970 by Walker and Company, a division of the Walker Publishing Company, Inc. Published simultaneously in Canada by The Ryerson Press, Toronto.

Library of Congress Catalog Card Number: 72-126122 / Typography by Lena Fong Hor

Printed in Japan

ISBN Trade, 0-8027-6084-8 / reinforced, 0-8027-6085-6